Felix,

The Mamas and Papas in this book
know that their little ones are special.
I want you to know that you will
always be special to me, and that
I will love you forever and ever
and always.

Weezy
8/8/14

You Are Special, Little One

NANCY TAFURI

DUCK POND PRESS • CONNECTICUT

LIBRARY OF CONGRESS CATALOGING-IN-PUBLICATION DATA
ISBN 978-0-9763369-1-4

The animals featured in this book include: lion and weaver bird; agama lizard;
black-prairie dog and prairie chicken; Camus pocket gopher; king penguin
and artic tern; crabeater seal; beaver; carp; and pickerel frog; dragonfly; eastern
meadowlark and New England cottontail; bumblebee; red fox and bobwhite quail;
racoon; and brown trout and common yellowthroat.

DUCK POND PRESS first edition published in 2013
10 9 8 7 6 5 4 3 2 1

Printed in Malaysia
The illustrations were painted in watercolors and inks.
The text is set in 22 point Iowan Bold.

To Cristina
and every child . . .
you are so special.

*O*n a hot savannah
under a shady tree,
a lion cub asks,
"How am I special?"

And Mama and Papa Lion reply,
"Dear little one,
with your dense, golden coat
and your deep, resounding purr,
you are so special,
and we will love you
forever and ever and always."

In a burrow opening
on a grassy plain,
a prairie dog pup asks,
"How am I special?"

And Mama and Papa Prairie Dog reply,
"Dear little one,
    with your keen, watchful eyes
    and your powerful legs for digging,
    you are so special,
    and we will love you
    forever and ever and always."

Atop an icy floe
on a snow-fringed sea,
a penguin chick asks,
"How am I special?"

And Mama and Papa Penguin reply,
"Dear little one,
with your soft, downy coat
and your swift, graceful swimming,
you are so special,
and we will love you
forever and ever and always."

High on their lodge
in a cool, clear pond,
a beaver kit asks,
"How am I special?"

And Mama and Papa Beaver reply,
"Dear little one,
   with your sleek, heavy fur
   and your large, webbed feet for diving,
   you are so special,
   and we will love you
   forever and ever and always."

Nestled in a thicket
by a farmland meadow,
a lark youngling asks,
"How am I special?"

And Mama and Papa Lark reply,
"Dear little one,
 with your bright yellow feathers
 and your light, cheerful song,
 you are so special,
 and we will love you
 forever and ever and always."

Deep in a tree trunk
by a woodland grove,
a fox cub asks,
"How am I special?"

And Mama and Papa Fox reply,
"Dear little one,
with your red, bushy tail
and your clever, nimble ways,
you are so special,
and we will love you
forever and ever and always."

In a grassy pasture
by a gently flowing stream,
a young child asks,
"How am I special?"

And Mama and Papa reply,
"Dear little one,
   with your warm, caring heart
   and your bright, curious mind,
   you are so special,
   and we will love you
   forever and ever and always."